The Starr Student

A HAPPY TAIL FROM THE GOOFY NEWFIE

Stephanie M. Kwisnek

PAGE PUBLISHING, INC.
New York, NY

First originally published by Page Publishing, Inc. 2016

ISBN 978-1-68213-948-6 (Paperback)
ISBN 978-1-68348-052-5 (Hard Cover)
ISBN 978-1-68213-949-3 (Digital)

Printed in the United States of America

Hi. My name is Starr.
Starr is short for Stephanie's Starry Night.
I am a Newfoundland dog – one of the biggest in the dog
world, but also one of the most gentle.

Mommy drives me to school, where I am the Starr Student! Well, Starr Student in training is more like it.

I am learning how to become a therapy dog so I can bring smiles and comfort to people I visit, including patients in hospitals.

A therapy dog also gives encouragement and confidence to those who may need just a little more help in learning how to read.

In school, I am learning how to listen and how to carry things – like a basket of flowers to brighten someone's day.

I am also learning how to walk like a lady to show everyone how friendly I am.

But school is not always fun and games.
"Starr, you better get up now or you will be late for school."

"I am not going to school today. I am just going to hide under my covers."

15

"But why? You love school," Mommy says.
"Not anymore," Starr replies. "Some people are mean."
"Why do you say that?" Mommy asks.

"Some of my friends were making fun of me," Starr cries. "They said I am too big to help people, and they were laughing at my feet!"

"You see, my feet point out, like a ballerina's. They are not straight, like my friends'.

It feels like everyone is always pointing and talking about my feet. I might be clumsy sometimes – like when I drop the flower basket by accident – and I might step on other people's feet when I trip – but I do not mean to do those things."

"That is okay Starr," Mommy says.
"You are kind and caring, and that is what matters.
I love you. I love your feet. You are my Starr!

"We do not look the same or act the same which makes
each and every one of us a star in our own, special way.
Now, let's go to school!"

Always remember - You are a Starr, too.
See you on our next Happy Tail adventure!

20

ABOUT THE AUTHOR

Stephanie's love of Newfoundlands brought her and Starr together and the beginning of a beautiful, loving companionship. Stephanie and Starr live in Arlington, Virginia, where Starr is living the diva-licious lifestyle of a pampered pup.

Stephanie has had Starr trained and certified as a therapy dog, and she works with children and adults of all ages around the Washington, D.C. metro area.

Starr brings joy and amazement to people everywhere she goes, and she even brings out the 'pawpawrazzi' who snap selfies with this gentle giant. Starr's 'pawsitive' attitude and sweet-natured personality have made her a four-footed local celebrity.

Both Stephanie and Starr are at their happiest when they're bringing smiles to other people. Stephanie is using her background in journalism and Starr's daily antics to create and share inspiring stories of Starr's happy tail adventures.

CPSIA information can be obtained
at www.ICGtesting.com
Printed in the USA
LVHW071957060721
692019LV00004B/9